If I Were an Alien

Published in 2009 by Windmill Books, LLC
303 Park Avenue South, Suite # 1280, New York, NY 10010-3657

Series Editor: Nick Turpin
Design: Robert Walster
Production: Jenny Mulvanny
Series Consultant: Gill Matthews

Publisher Cataloging Data

French, Vivian
        If I were an alien / by Vivian French ; illustrated by Lisa Williams.
                p.   cm. – (Get set readers)
        Summary: A little boy wishes he were an alien in outer space, while a
space alien wishes he were a little boy on Earth.
        ISBN 978-1-60754-267-4
        1. Extraterrestrial beings—Juvenile fiction   [1. Extraterrestrial beings—
Fiction   2. Stories in rhyme]   I. Williams, Lisa, 1970-   II. Title   III. Series
        [E]—dc22

Manufactured in the United States of America

If I Were an Alien

by Vivian French

illustrated by Lisa Williams

alphabet
soup
an imprint of
WINDMILL
BOOKS
New York

EASY
FRENCH V

I wish I were an alien floating up in space.

I'd fly around the planets...

8

13

I wish I were a boy on Earth
and didn't live in space.
I wouldn't have these
tentacles, I'd have
a human face.

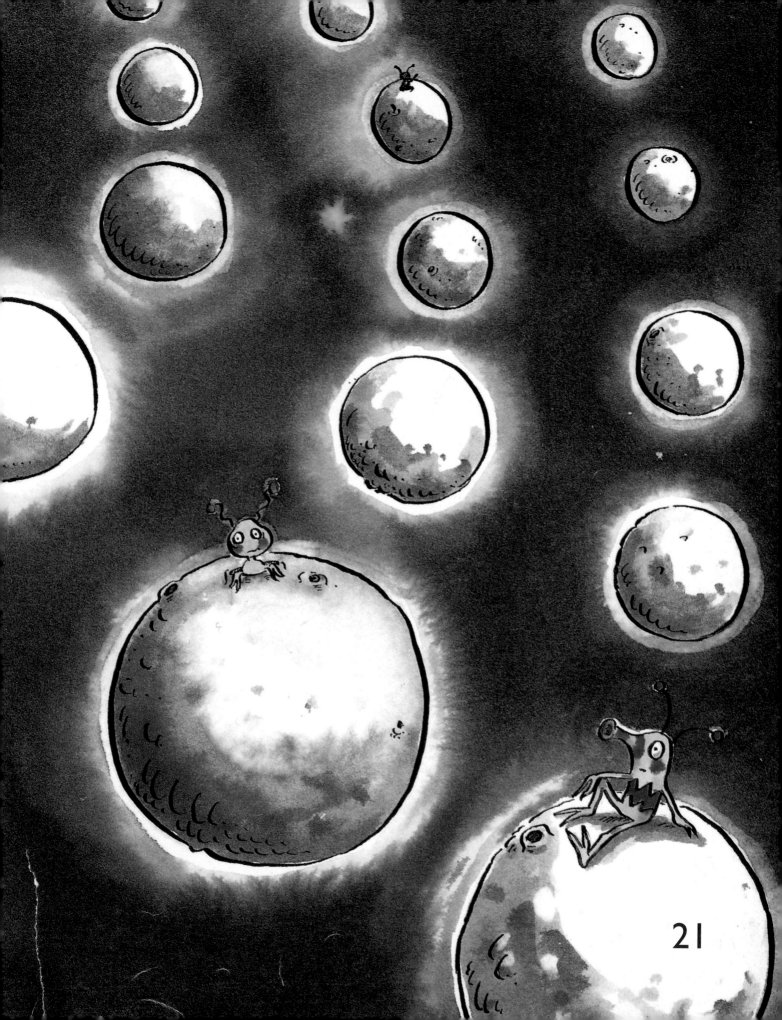

I want to ride on buses...

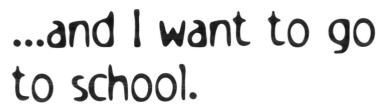

31

For more great fiction and nonfiction, go to www.windmillbks.com.